Dedicated to

The Romanian hippies from the '70's,
who showed me an alternate path of beauty and freedom
when the road was dark.

Also by Ioana Cosma

The Psychogeography of Love (Silver Bow Publishing) 2021
In Aevo (Silver Bow Publishing) 2020
By the Book (The European Institute Press) 2020

For the Love
of
Woodstock

by

Ioana Cosma

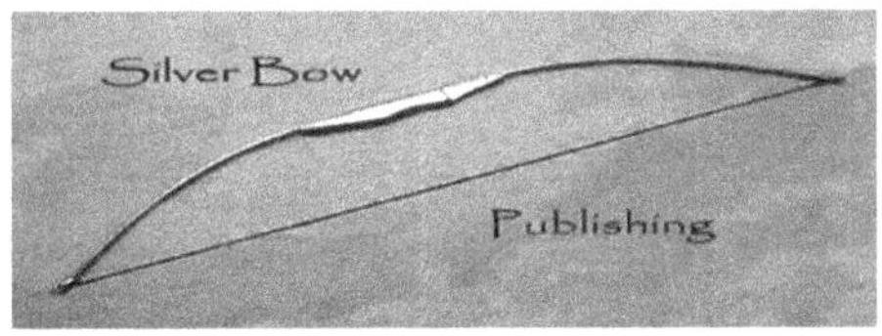

720 Sixth Street, Unit #5
New Westminster, BC
V3L 3C5
CANADA

Title: For the Love of Woodstock
Author: Ioana Cosma
Publisher: Silver Bow Publishing
Cover Design: "Major 7th Dimension" painting by Candice James
Layout and editing: Candice James

www.silverbowpublishing.com
info@silverbowpublishing.com
ISBN: 978-1-77403-193-3 paperback
ISBN: 978-1-77403-194-0 epub

Library and Archives Canada Cataloguing in Publication

Title: For the love of Woodstock / by Ioana Cosma.
Names: Cosma, Ioana, 1979- author.
Identifiers: Canadiana (print) 20220133115 | Canadiana (ebook) 20220133816 | ISBN 9781774031933
   (softcover) | ISBN 9781774031940 (EPUB)
Subjects: LCGFT: Poetry.
Classification: LCC PR9170.R63 F67 2022 | DDC 821/.92—dc23

Foreword

Bless that man! In 1969, Max Yasgur rented out 600 acres of his farm near Bethel, New York to the largest gathering of youth ever in history. He was happy to host, what he thought, would be about 50,000 young people on his farm. Instead, Mr. Yasgur, ended up shocked; 500,000 hippies showed up to celebrate freedom, love and music on his land.

We were a lost and unhappy generation of teenagers. Many of us had run away from home, and many had no home to go to. We started taking psychedelics to escape and in our escape, found many inner treasures, which *Ioana Cosma* has captured beautifully in this poetry; a deep understanding of what this generation was searching for.

Three glorious days of love, peace and music; we were in heaven! Some of the biggest and best rock and roll bands played, while hippies dreamed and swayed in the field: The Grateful Dead, Jimi Hendrix, Janis Joplin with her raunchy, drawn out vocal chords; Richie Havens, and so many more who are looked at today as Rock and Roll idols of the past.

We showed the world peace was possible. We showed the world how much more beautiful and free life could be. Our youth came out of Woodstock with a dream to change the world!!

It was an era unlike any other mankind had or has since experienced. The psychological and emotional growth was exponential ... it was as if we had stolen this wisdom from a future time. We wanted to share it, but adults did not want to listen.

We lived, loved, made music, made love, built communities we called communes, and we learned to live together in a supportive and loving way. Those of our generation who did not sell out to corporate America on down the years, still await the coming of this world we know was possible. Instead, they ignored us.

Though they ignored us, we brought forward with us a word that would bring us the peace of meditation; a word that would remind us always of how close we came to building the society we dreamed of; a word that could take us back to this way of being within us whenever we wished to visit ~ and this word is *Om*. ~ **Deborah L. Kelly, *Author of Songs of the North, Glass Houses***

Table of Contents:

Prologue

Soundtracks

Tracks

The Maestro

I followed the night orchestra
like an orphaned child of heaven.
The muted rivers pushed me onwards
while the operatic dahlias fluttered like flute song.
It was the bread of misfits and the chant of salt.

An angel's scar plummeting from towers
with shards of glass inside a mosaic of crossroads:
I went back and forthwith the music
that crystalized from silence and stoning
on a field that fed on a sparrow's hope.

The tune was a trumpet's call to the arms of forgiveness
the words were scarce; the weight of hollow-sounding cymbals
but love poured in like from the Samaritan woman's fingers;
the daunting light had the smell of warmed clay.

They sang of man's ploy and the forgotten sounds of fury,
the marks of time and timelessness on unprepared hearts,
it seemed playful and fun save for a deathlike pallor of the mind
as it gives way to a vagrant guide.

At length, I perceived the Maestro:
a gentle giant who slept for weeks in an infant's cradle,
he was a bit everywhere
and his garments had the appearance of romantic songs.
He'd completed his tremendous work of love.

Then I began to sing in tune like a choir child
free from the bonds of fear and doom.
The unleashed rivers followed me in my tracks
crossing constellations of bows and carillons,
the words that stuck in my mind
had the name of daydreamers that pray.

The conductor began to sing
and his hand let the stick go.

Soundtracks

12

All That Blues
(Based on Tim Hardin's "Blues all Over my Ceiling")

We wore the blues like we'd invented them
like two kids in swings when one was going up,
the other down. I drowned and you soared.
We both fought and made peace with the walrus.

You said we were under the spell of the moon
but I begged to differ:
even the hatchling moon had cast us out
like aborted eggs.
I stared at the sun a bit too long
while you were screaming
from deep inside the well.

Can this go on forever?
The bluesman says it can.
Even music has freaks
and we were the lunatics from underground
striking the chords on the thin red line
between the high and the low.

So I stopped right then and there
knowing I would never meet you
caught in our frail equilibrium
lest another should fall,

We sent signals like distant space stations
to the blue earth

Hatching the Sound

I left my keys on the timorous ground
together with my dreams; they jangled anxiously
in their timid expectation of a kiss.
Stay there, you shouted, loud enough
to make my white shirt shiver,
my body feel your might.

So you left.
I stayed stranded for God knows how long
on the carillon sea headphones in my ears, drowning.
I posed no opposition for waves are soft and mild
they always take you somewhere –
better than my nowhere.

The dissolution of love is like wax that melts
on a bronze candlestick;
it leaves behind deformed traces
that no onecan restore.
It is an overexposed color photograph
that dilutes like the salt of the earth
to give the taste of drowning.

I think I heard you hatching a sound
from a boy's toy box
but it mostly feels like dreaming
like looking through a transparent glass
and not seeing anything:
the horizon of opacity,
the dismal diminution of indigo
from aging ink.

Sell 'Em
(Based on Melanie's "Tuning my Guitar")

She never quite emerged, although she was prepared
the canopy of song was too thick for submissive breathing
so she took to tuning her guitar like a distanced cousin
she discovered on the trip from cradle to grave.

The long ordeal was almost over
she'd spared her dreams but not her soul
that had been sold by a drunken pirate
to the children of revelation.
Inside the tower and ontoglassy pavements
she saw the reflection of sin.

Of all the people who once had gathered
inside the invisible church that sang for redemption.
She tuned her guitar once more
to the sounds of the orchestra of clearings
seen in visions by prophets and priests of peace.

She tried to breathe once more but couldn't.
The idol'sfoot had fallen flat
on the fragile temple of love.
She was barely alive when they found her.
They all applauded: the performance
of holy doves.

Get Together
(Based on Chet Powers/Dino Valenti's "Get Together")

There's ivy tied to her hair
caressing his ecstatic look.
There are children that got the answer
way before they learnt to ask.

I sometimes see visions of freedom and beauty
but they're blurrier now and they've lost their luster.
I sometimes chant with the freed people of Babylon
but there's always the man who asks for his son's ransom.

In the light, the contour light there's peace of mind
and there's a crowd that escaped
bathing and blessed like a suckling babe.

To these eccentric sights we tied our hopes
and aspirations of kids who'd been numbered,
sold and cut to the bone
by those invisible hands that sift chaff from wheat
as if the souls were something to eat.

Get together, even for a moment in time,
humanity devoid of pretension and greed
born from the choirs that call for a man,
a woman and their blossom.

With a Little Help from My Friends
(Based on Joe Cocker's "A Little Help from My Friends")

The monsoon tide blew hard and heavy.
The lonesome heart gave way naturally;
it was a rip and a mere rumor
but it tore, to pieces, the sail and the careen.

The night fell on the hollow ground..
Bare breathing was the only sound.
A muted seagull's scream, a hologram of dreams
that sip into reality like venom.

There was no question of returning
and no shore in sight
for the shores had been vanished.
Black water was blacker and blacker like solid blood.

Invisible hands
started to sew the sailcloth
mend the careen wood
the ship emerged
from the dark abyss holding on barely,
frail, but held on by the power of wings.

She took wind and flew past the night time
into the soft horizon that shifted
as she approached a liquid peninsula,
a vagrant country for the forever homeless.

Going Up the Country
(Canned Heat)

I may have not been a hippie
He may have not been a hit
But the night blind covered our nakedness
like stained sheet.

I may not have been sober.
He may not have been a saint,
but the fragrance we left in our tracks
was like the essence of anointed feet.

I may have left for Paris.
He may have stayed for Helen.
Our feet were dissolving
like waves that unfurl stories.

I may have been too young.
He may have been too eager.
Upstate they found a ghost
that played our song for hours.

I may be older now.
He may be sweet or sour,
but once we took the hint of light
from clumsy hands that toil.

The Ritual
(Based on Santana's "Soul Sacrifice")

Bless the return, each summer, of the sons that sing,
of the dancing daughter of the blasted field,
the crowds that call for blood and for the life of lambs
invoking rain and sorrow with their make-up masks.

Bless the whip that lashes like flames on witches' pyres, .
the stained soil, the dirty water,
the maiden's shame coming back
with nostalgia in the eyes of men
each hallowed midnight that rings like a choir.

Bless the hand that beats
and the hand that rips shirts off proud shoulders:
it took its time like a soldier of fortune
to protect stubs from wings
and shards from eyes like windows.
It will one day rest on a breathless chest.

Bless the blood-drinking people
and the brothers that kill scapegoats of intolerance
vestals of defeat keep singing their return,
their glorious hymn to the gods with feet of clay
and hearts of soot.

What's Wrong
(Based on Sweetwater's eponymous song)

We've been closing our eyes to tongue-tied kids
and beats from the pulpitex-cathedral:
an ex-cathedral of rancorous sermons
for the faint of heart,
for the children of crystal.

First come the eyes whose vision dims slowly.
Then the ears close to the words and the truth.
Last comes the mouth silenced for good
like a deer bowing its neck to the wolf's bite.

Felling and felling all living things
like a manic blindman
who wants to make his way
to the heart of things
because the outside is sick and dull.
But the heart is failing
and the mind is blunt.

The introverts wear knives in their sleeves.
The frustrated teens a rifle on their shoulders;
they will never appease the beast;
they will blow torches on the waters of dreams.

90's Hippie
(Based on Bert Sommer's "Jennifer")

This one goes to wearing trapeze jeans in the nineties
to getting beaten by rappers and cops,
to being thrown out of bars,
to leaving your lover on a May day.

She cruised to the black sea on a train of desire.
she talked to the spirits and stars in her sleep
while coral boats were afloat
by her lashes that drowned
and colibris touched her hair like strings.

Stuck in a station that led north of home
she combined hope and vodka
to open a doorof perception.
She saw the Indian god
and the mother of puppets
but she never found herself again.

Last time I saw her
she was planting flowers in a small garden.
She was wearing a summer hat
over her long greying hair.
he looked distracted and apathetic
but her long hands were no longer shaking
like wings in the open air.

The Carpenter's Wife
(Based on Tim Hardin's "If I Were A Carpenter")

There's dust entangled in the hair on his arms
sparkling with sweat and sorrow.

There's a new child
in a barn somewhere
for each guilty nail
in a wall of flowers.

His eyes are blunt
and his manners are steel blue.
I begged him to linger
in the clement hour.

He went on to build,
from his palms like cradles,
a house for those
who fed on roses.

I admired his work
but I kept my silence.

I just baked black bread
and smiled to the icons.

The Beauty in You
(Based on Melanie's "Beautiful People")

The beauty in her
was the beauty in submerged cities of convenience.
They lie hidden from sight for centuries
until a mad diver stumbles upon them
in his search for starfish and pearls.

Closed eyes, she travelled in the same subway
until a handshake began to signify more than a handshake.
A grin more than a grin. Crossed legs more than crossed legs.
Like a choreography of symbols weaving up a ladder.

First, she saw the other story dimly
then it became sonorous like vibrating air.
She could hear the music inside the skin
touching the iron bar, the diverting eye,
falling blankly on a commercial for sunglasses.

As she cleared the soot off tired workers' foreheads,
the make-up off humble secretaries' cheeks,
the ink off little children's fingers,
she perceived their beauty and also their defeat.
Her own now to behold
like a love to admire from a distance and with care.

The scolding mothers became the tides that drown
under the force of the moon.
The wars, a parody of puppets that play on a stage set.
Beauty destroyed temporarily.

As the world recovered its beauty,
she became aware of her own appearance:
resembling a dragonfly that ogles a flower in bloom
and softly touches the watery surface with its blue back.
The gentleness of everything.

I Live One Day at a Time
(Based on Joan Baez's "I Live One Day at a Time")

The dervish waved goodbye
to the fields of rye and plaster
that had sung with her the life-gushing chant
rising with the force of a helix above and beyond
mind's waters that now gave way.

She-dervish, she-flute afloat
still hanging tight
to the blade of grass like no other
to the dangling step in movement
and in a gap-between minutes and God.

Pacing at a time; pacing profusely the sinewy grid
made up of days that never wait
a list, a startled heart that lingers
just enoughto see the kids grow up one more night.

The dervish once stopped spinning
but it was for the smitten sunflowers
like sundials of heaven on earth.
Now was everywhere
and anyhow was sometimes
a flutter of lashes touched by the gusts
of never-ending Decembers.

The Day I Die
(Based on Quills' "Drifting")

25

Come right this death adrift, this hollow hound,
the copper coins on this child's ivory lashes.
Come fight the right of nature to oblivion
like every trembling thing in air and fire.

Death's randomness
has nothing on this vagrant soul
that has battled the windmills of parody
and despises that which has bathed carelessly
in the waters of Tartar
and hewn wings out of melting wax.

Drifting is dying a little
on the stage of noncommittal sinners;
a passage through life like a duck in a pond.
It feels a bit Buddhist,
so cool for this age of comfort
when in truth it's like a ship tied to a harpsichord.

The Mellow Blues '
(Based on John Sebastian's "Rainbows all over Your Blues")

Like the blue moon swinging,
the heron pecking in the neon light,
the sun softly surrendering to the accruing night,
she sold her house for rainbows
and for a wanton heart.

She knew old age would come
with a sense of sugary taste in her bold bones;
in her tempestuous blood that breathed out;
in her voice that now faltered and stumbled a bit.

She didn't know that the planet was blue
and that blue was the orchard blue
the heart of palms
that touched beautiful locks of hair
like the liquid screen of the machine
that fed her dreams.

When she climbed up the rainbow staircase
she finally perceived the blueness of lover's thighs
as they drown in the amnesiac crowds,
pole dancing on a subway that takes them away...
just takes them away.

Lovin' is Sin and The Holy Ghost
(Based on Sam Hunt's "Sinnin with You")

They tied the Holy Ghost
and brought her here to witness
the decay of soul
the body betrayed;
the chaff of limbs shattered
in the aftermath of concupiscence.

She bathed her belly brown
 from the clay of rivers that never drown a soul.
He, famished, watched her:
eyes weary and replenished
a baptism that sets free the lonely.

They were never lost
but somehow they were found lying
like Teuton lovers.
A shield between their ribcages,
shorn monk hair, their clipped wings
and their dispossessed fingers.

It was never a sin but the story goes like this;
Dante saw them on the steps of a burning temple
where they erase love.
Forgetting and loving a little less each morning
with the help of the powers that be
and at God's command.

Who You Are
(Based on a song by The Incredible String Band)

That moment of realization, I
ike a droplet of stained glass
in the vaults of time's misgivings,
when who you are is who you once were,
a mix of disgust and fear in your dried-up mouth
that has forgotten the taste of figs.

Can you love yourself then or shatter yourself to pieces
to the galaxies complicitous with the roundabout theme?
Maybe find a third way from the knowledge your father gave you
where you finally make a joke that doesn't kill or hurt?

The martial law rules over all fallen souls
and drunken hearts welcome this lucidity
then a friend in these times of fakeness
makes it your real mask
and, without parting lips, speak out:
you, the real you.
Who you were and who you are ...
holding in the universe.

A Story Untold
(Based on Jefferson Airplane's "Eskimo Blue Day")

"But the human nature
doesn't mean shit to a tree"
yet it might get an idea the minute it gets felled:
all lies in the decisiveness of the cut.

Our stories are like that
made of tree mass and black tar:
a heavy-loaded shotgun we use
to aim at no one.

The stories of trees
are written and told in darkened rooms
by men that have felt the graze
of timber on their hardened skins.

All they have is this freeze-frame,
an impression that lies
between evidence and smoke,
where the former is traceless
and the latter pregnant ...
:a story untold.

Easy Peasy
(Based on Crosby, Still and Nash's "Wooden Ships")

Faster than fury
then add the horizon,
the shoreline that divides hope from hearkening
in the end,
the black boat of stone set sail
away from the silver silhouettes.

Hidden by night, the laughter subsided
muffled by those waves of denial
that wash away newborn shells,
a remanence from the time
when men hadn't heard the "division bell".

She glided and glowed a subtle light
from the dreams of men
that were her cargo and breath.
They had exchanged their fitting in clothes
for a sound that flickers
until it becomes white noise.

Where do you take these hippies,
these berry-eaters, these meek rebels?
"Elsewhere", was the answer,
for"else" is what remains
when "where" has become a territory:
the silver silhouettes that play.

She-Icarus
(Based on "Flying High Bird", Richie Havens)

When wax wanes like fearful flowers
and you feel your neck crack
under the weight of the sun
the beauty of it
before the most beautiful pupil falls
on the weariest eye.

Flying, rooted in the gravity of flight,
the bird of clay, the grey bird of feathers,
drowning all the calmness,
zigzagging the crumbling light.

The cruel design in such a contradictory mind
her own fata morgana to stare at
in a mirror the unfolds night and more night.
The recurrence of tension and *trauma*.

She covered it all
in a canopy of sound and serenity.
The sirens howled
and the walls once more trembled
but still she carried this cross
across the most unforgiving skies.

The Turn of the Spider
(Based on Sweetwater's "Crystal Spider")

Have you seen the might and glory
in a spider's crystal climb?
The agony and ecstasy of creating nothingness:
nets that burn the inside.

Dear spider, please forgive me.
I have not known how to feel for you.
You knew nothing about love
so you unwove your soul like a stripper.

Itsy-bitsy, –.
you make it look easy
when, in truth,
it feels:
like three Golgothas,
like a miner,
like a soldier
like the salt
and like ...
the blasted son.

The Tongue-Tied Child
(Based on Tim Hardin's "Speak like a Child")

Her mind was an ocean floor
submerged and silent like the seashells.
Pearls hung heavy and pregnant.

The words wouldn't come to her mouth
although she'd seen so many splendid worlds.
It felt a bit like lying flat-belly on the ground
like a seal that cannot reach the shore.

The mutiny of words inside her tiny framework –
they were loud and furious
those tongue-tied words.
She clasped the chords of the lyre
Orpheus had dropped on the floor.

At first it was a little trifle,
a *je-ne-sais quoi* you cannot put your finger on.
The symbol of the speechless mouth
and eyes that have seen the end of the world.

She transmitted airwaves from the whale's belly,
the gramophone was on repeat.
The life aquatic and sedated fit her,
like handmade mittens
made of entangled wool.

Re/Generation
(Based on The Who's, "My Generation")

I dig my generation because it's in-between
the desperate and the protected.
our flaws and faults blend with our great desire.

The Who said it best
it's the hippies who will win
in the unwritten book of history redeemed
one day like a serene sleep under a blue baldachin
children of crowds, crows and corrosion.

We grazed the punk and graffitied the rock
on stone walls tall enough to hide the falling façades.
We tempted the devil but he tempted us first
a bitter laughter at the end. Who cares?

My generation is flying on a comet of hopelessness
that feels like home;
it plays hide-and-seek with laughing buddhas
and boasts flamboyantly
the slashing, wounding song – who cares?

it's the hippies who will win.

The Fiddler on the Tin Roof
(Based on The Who's "Fiddle About")

There is a fiddler on a tin roof
who stopped his heartbeat to hear the sound of Mercury
as he filtered his mind through the wind
progressing through air with each fickle note.

There are blisters on the soles of his feet
and lichen roots on his faltering shoulders.
There is a traded bead for each of his sins
and frying fish that stare from a pan of enamel.

The fiddler flew the fiddler grew the fiddler knew
the cadence of the seasons and of nightfall.
The climb was harsh but he longed for the Everest
because his parents told him he was crazy.

He knew by heart the score of hell and heaven
he tried to save a few but lost himself in the process
Completeness, beauty, another chord to strike:
Oh, how I loved the fiddler, but we grew apart.

The Lingering Haze
(Based on Jimmy Hendrix's "Purple Haze")

Flying off to another shore
maybe one day
the ship that sailed away will come back.
Maybe not;
It's the mystery of connection with flowers
that awakens the dead from their innocent slumber.

The purple haze left its stain on your lips
and your eyes became like puddles of alabaster
from a fairytale by Gaiman told repeatedly
on a winter night to the devotee children of light.

The slow-mo of lovers semi-drunken on silken skin
the days melted into one and the nights diluted
like ink on a white shirt worn by a man
who'd forgotten the first time he'd cried.

Dreams haze in hazel eyes and wallow
in the design and embrace of seagulls,
on a foggy shore
where anthracite stones linger
away from the cavalcade of days.

When She Was a Gypsy Woman
(Based on Jimmy Hendrix's "Gypsy Woman")

Away from the fire she plotted with mugs,
who'd fallen from heaven like acrobats on gossamer ropes
and landed on thin blades of grass.
Gypsy woman, they said, come sit by our side.

She wore Alhambra flowers and Seraglio beads,
her hair was pinned in dark nets of lace,
her feet were small but never static
she danced to the Moors' beat.

She'd left the caravan and her lot
for a thief of hearts and horses
who drank like a Kazakh soldier
and ravished the land and women for gold.

She washed his clothes in cold mountain water
till they became blue-white
like the skin on her hallowed hands
that wore rings from her father's descendants
up to the last forlorn heirloom.

When she last saw him,
he was sharpening a knife,
he looked at her and cursed her
but she couldn't hear.

She heard the mugs' music
played on guitar
and saw soot pouring
from his tourmaline eyes.

You and Me
(Based on Richie Haven's "From the Prison")

My second image of a prison
was Peter's night escape from chains.
It always spoke to my tremendous need for freedom
matched only by the birds that fly alone.

You and me are a pretty dance trauma
slowly peeling off the layers of painted faces
reminiscent of an Etruscan portrait
combining out-of-this-world beauty with death.

You say it's like a prison here
but you have Pete's ways
I only have this patchwork canvas I got from grandma
and my Urmuz tube to trade stamps with you.

Let's make a pact:
I'll die when you forgive the fairies.

Stranger than Fiction
(Based on Richie Haven's "I'm a stranger here")

Whoever said fiction is strange was lying.
She never saw the soft tendrils as they go to work,
the night sky in a woman's heart
or the sad children's eyes in their worlds apart.

Must've been a poet. They say poets lie.
Anyway, the best things I know about life
are from books written by men
who swore to speak the truth
and nothing but the truth:
Go challenge Dostoyevsky, for instance.

It was stranger than fiction when my body was put to
released and marked like a slaughterhouse beast.
How hated the blood heritage;
how disconsolate the black widow
and her two penny-opera of love.

Fiction was never strange to me;
it was my true home.
I cannot find chaos of mind here
I shouldn't be expected to abhor the ones
that were tender to me:
the night and story nurses.

Tracks

42

The Grey and Black Words

She counted all her unsaid words:
they were black and grey
like skies in the expectation of storm
like houses from an industrial town
covered in soot and snow.

She sat upright carrying this heavy burden
for silenced words have the gravity of sunsets,
the ambiguity of greying hair
and the opacity of tar
like the decay of sparrows' cheer in winter.

She started writing them in an old notebook
with black ink on the greying pages,
she started hesitantly at first
but then her hands wrote with a vengeance
like they'd waited a whole lifetime for the occasion.

When she finished, she felt tired but content,
her little secret story now released
after fifty years of torment
she'd kept behind her heavy eyelids:
it was not all black and white, after all.

Scarlet Ida

When Ida was a little girl
she wrought wreaths of thistles and ivy;
she cut short the hair of her dolls
and dyed their lips in black enamel.

The day she died
she saw a golden wheatfield and the reapers.

Ida came to this world without hope or fear.
At fourteen she drank like a Russian Kazakh
she smoked clove cigarettes and gave her body freely
to any passer-by really, it didn't matter, anyway.

One day she knew she'd had too much
so she decided to vanish
like whitewash watercolor from an old painting.
The mirror where she beheld her grotesque face and garments
reflected nothing of her troubled, frail soul.

On sedimentary rock she landed
lending her body to the lunar limelight.
She was clad in clouds for clouds are mercy.
She summersaulted into galaxies and constellations
that drew a map of the inverted world of slumber.

The make-up was fading
little by little like ancient pyrography
that was no longer needed.
Her cheeks recovered a rosy hue
that matched the scarlet dusk, the crimson dawn,
the lipstick and the blood on her slit wrists.

Give Peace a Chance

My generation was fed on music
like baby bees on nectar and pollen.
We became adults when we were younger
and kids when we grew older.
The music fed the fire in us until the fire became blaze
and blaze a torch that turned to light.

They say music unites.
 I found my best friends through music
and music is the sweetest of my friends
I sang and sang and sang
till I became a river that went to the sea
and then I learnt peace from the blue abyss.

We are too different
not to have to be united through music;
too tormented and fueled by life's force.
Music is where the best of our aspirations meet.
Music will last and unite us in an angels' choir.

As I write poetry
I am aware that this, our art,
will give way to this kind of music,
because it is graceful and compelling and so pure

"Give peace a chance"
will be our generation's song.

The Partisan's Way Back Home

It was a late summer day when he came back
eyes weary with brown circles
like he'd cried a mountain river
like he had travelled to the middle of the earth and back
with a frail heart that had only known terror.

He'd lost a few brothers in the battle,
he had seen children die and the fright in their eyes
he'd hidden in barns and drunk cows' milk from the udder.
All this time he wanted to die.

There was warmth and love in nature
and insects were humming a mellow tune.
He walked as if asleep in a dream
but his steps knew the way back;
they followed the hearth's call
and his wife's lament.

At first, he was speechless and senseless like marble
he beheld his children with a dead man's eyes
something was forever destroyed in the back of his mind
and he looked at his family like a cripple a prop.

One day he woke up and the sun was shining.
He saw his ironed blue shirt
on the back of a chair
an image relapsed from the vaults of time
of when his mother would feed him berries and milk.

That day he embraced his children
and waved adieu to his comrades,
he made the sign of the cross in the earth
and hid it under of patch of daffodils.

He then took his wife in his arms
and began to speak.

The Fragrant Tomb

When Xin Zhui woke from her age-old slumber,
she noticed her dress had caught a bit of dust,
a little patina of green luster,
as though she'd crossed the marshes of the staring dead.

She watched her husband apathetically and calmly.
She'd never loved him or so she thought.
At last released from the bonds of marriage
she left her jade ring behind in the tomb.

She began to roam the cities surrounded by stardust,
a few moonlit tabernacles where she wedded strangers,
the tents of warriors who play with foals
and the cloisters of sultans' odalisques.

She felt appeased at last
and watched her ivory complexion
in a brass mirror.
Her raven hair had become purple
like night skies lit by the chandeliers
from an age where she longed to become
a nascent star.

Her trails left behind an inexplicable fragrance
that clad the city walls in dreams of roses and ivy.

She never felt the scent ...
but it is rumored ...
they found her with a perfume bottle in her hand.

Can I Compare Thee

Unique and lonely like a semi-precious stone
he lay in folds of apathy and torment.
He was beyond comparison and yet
the world had turned him into the infinitesimal.

Ad infinitum
the universe might lose its vocation for comparison:
a will to tie the knot between the unsaid
and the cheating visibility of matter
as though we were made to withstand
the weight of the beauty of others.

He was beyond comparison and peaceful.
The realm of things no longer had dominion over him.
Beneath his feet the kingdom of bonds that stifle
in spite of their loveliness and their struggle against it..

Blood Lines

There are blood lines in the songs you sing
just like there are ribs on the skin of dandelion leaves.
There is restlessness of the limbs and the sore of words
that were never meant to remain.

Take it from there from your non-winning non-combat
and wrap it up in the silver layers of magic and dream.
Maybe think about the throbbing pulse of a heron
as it takes flight for the first time.

Icarus is long dead
and so is his father's impossible dream.

But as you dive deep into those storylines
of loved ones that had to,
remember for a second
how in the best of worlds
you won the fight
with the worst of demons:
            the daylight dreamer
            and the never-ending blue.

Spanish Summer

I see them now clearly: sitting cross-legged
in their oh so graceful pose
on white garlanded chairs in the
the two men-lovers of the land,
the two enormous angels
who embraced the city, me and blindfolds.

Lorca and Alberti and the aftertaste of summer in Granada
cats lazing under striped shades
oranges oozing the wine of concupiscence
beautified bodies prolonging what may have remained
from the afternoon storm.

Static passages zigzagging like busy cars
on the belt of the Hesperides that summer
came with sad presages and complicitous smiles
cast to each other one hundred years away.

I sat by your statues.
My poetry book made no nonsense
like it knew you by heart.

I gazed at the entrance that was transforming
yellow to goldsilver to fondant blue
like the memory I keep in my heart
of the fairness of you,
a drop of summer nostalgia on the ebony *ruelas*
where I still seek lost traces of you.

The Rain, the Forest

When did it all become industry?
When did it begin to rain?
After sorrow or before an apple core
was not thrown in a classroom
wounded by a blond child's first harrowing cry?

When did we become killers?
When did we start to die?
Was it after the first fall from the asphyxiating sky
or before they told you... you were ugly and blue?

Your knives slashed the precarious heart valve
that fed on day's crumbles like a prisoner from Mars.
She came to your party pristine, mad and pretty,
He was all eyes that were painted on his surreal leather jacket.

She'd crossed the Valley of Tears
before she learnt how to pull a trigger;
how to kiss a dead man.

He held her hand through all this
and after became a big star
in the industry of life's martyrdom.

The Dream of Stardust

Under the dust that flew like ravens
from her dress of winter,
from her hands of clover,
they still lay dormant but happy to awaken
all the past morning glories of the sons that wander.

They were too many to count and too few to compare.
They rose all at once like hatchlings
from turquoise egg shells cracking a smile
that looked like rosebush on her freckled cheek.

She danced awhile to their midnight stories
and read them tales in return
of when the moon still glittered
like mica bits on a ceramic vase she'd seen
on her grandmother's macramé mantelpiece.

Was it the '70's or 3040
when she took the wanderers into a tiny hollow
where they aligned like lead toy soldiers
half-seriously preparing for a wage less war
where nobody would win, not even stardust.

Scratch That!

53

Did you hear the screech?
It pounded puffs of smoke into the frosty air
where a Cinderella of one too many shoes
lost her way once more for a debonair dream.

Life is sweet and life is scary.
She thought one last time of Keats and Shelley,
dead companions of old,
staring blankly from the gallows.

It was a scratch night for the operatic patient
etherized once more on ethyl and opium.

"Que sera, sera", she stuttered.
"Scratch that! "she yelled.

"Oh! My heel is broken!" she screamed.

The Pigeon

I kept my eyes on you
like a samurai on a felled brick.
I was little and scared yet I kept my cool.
You and freedom were my first composition topic.
The first eccentric beings I'd seen in my whole life.

You danced with me in circles
in front of Pompidou museum
reminding me of the times
you accompanied me in the park.
at times you looked like silent observers,
watchers from above narrowing my path
with every single step from the sky down to earth
in smaller and smaller circles
up until the last sigh
into the new light of beginnings from paintings
where you held angels' robes
and Mary's wreath of olive leaves.

You were bound to be set free one day ....
like me.

Poets are Liars
(Revisited)

They say all poets are liars
because they lack the philosophers' lucidity;
they veil and alter at the whim of imaginationa tall tale
borrowed from men's suffering.

But poets see and sense a truth hidden from perception
like stars afar lit by a telescope of wonder.
"Everything is illuminated" in their skies of holy
in which they bathe like fish released from hooks.

The meaning they unveil
may remain obscure even to them:
the most fatal attractions of stars
like painted glassworks;
their words are purified and tainted
by the world below and above.

Rimbaud spent a "season in hell"
and emerged blameless and pale –
are poets absolved of the mortal sins?
A life on the altar of grace and despair
to make room for the light
that shone in the first day.

M.A.S.H. Up

Mankind needed M.A.S.H.
like it needed Mahatma Gandhi,
the zealots and the anarchists,
the ones that sing the blues
who go out and about the world
like minstrels of opposition
to the roaring laughter of gods
that play dice on the land.

It needed not so serious doctors
and Klingers and Radars
showing that love takes the unintrusive eye,
the blood and tear stained white gowns
washed by the hands of nurses that cry in their sleep.

They say laughter's the best response to cruelty in tragedy
but they started to laugh only in the twentieth century
Greek heroes were devoured by the venom of vileness
and the Romantic poets died young and sad.

Mankind needed M.A.S.H.
because it was absurd to keep crying,
because war, like all wayward sons, needed a correction.
The irony of the invading victim, the laughter of the doomed
plotting a story of vengeance on the intolerant and cruel.

We didn't see the carnage, we didn't see the fight
but we saw the wounded accruing as though on a bloody chart.
Hawkeye and Hunnicutt keeping the quiet vigil
with alcohol and love, far from the maddening crowd.

The Monks' Garden

Lavender fields by the Abbaye des Lereins,
a fragrance like the ancient sea
kissing the whitewash cliffs
from which we watched
the sun making love to the land.

the cloisters were dreaming in prim petals and wineas
the twelve of us feasted underneath orange trees
our eyes the color of purple from the lavender fields
our long hair tied to the Assumption song of birds.

The lavender loves and blesses the land;
it conspires with the tall cypress trees
and the discrete monks:
a poetic story
whispered by the sweet theologian
serving the land and us.

Me, Sparrow

Me, sparrow, arrow warrior in time,
Philoctetes, entrancer, dancer,
mythopoeticstance of minimum intrusion,
cherishing a puddle of water
on an early May morning.

Traversing the high seas,
the storms and prairies
sparrow wonder
sparrow glory
keeping its balance
while sleeping on a branch smiling,
with all its black and brown feathers,
to the new day.

She is the Son of God

She is the son of God
full of grace and compassion.
She wears a Gavroche hat that's too large
and smokes clove cigarettes.

She lives in Paris and Berlin three times a year
and has a lover in each harbour like a mariner.
She keeps an iguana pet in her sequined bed.

She is an entertainer and a host of hungry spirits
come to feast on human pain and sorrow.
She accommodates them with a graceful smile.

When the night falls she turns into a man,
a dandy who likes gambling and wine and women too,
provided they come equipped with a rose and gun.

Like her brother she likes to hang out
with lepers and sinners,
to have her feet washed
by strangers with myrrh.
She takes no hostages
yet she would never kill.

She is the son of God.
The missing link
in the story of creation,
Neither Lilith nor Eve
but the one
who was forgiven
and forgave.

Either/Or

When I open,
crack and fall
in the hands of ill-willed fate
I see things anew again
and I wonder at the world.

When I open round the edges
there's a slight sound like a knock
like a shy guest who hopes to vanish
by the time the door's unlocked.

Round the edges into darkness
I may hope to live or die
either in a frying pan with sausage
or as Leda the swan.

The Seventies' Songs of Innocence

The pill, the wine, the half-baked bread,
the tear gas and the wooden language
to stifle your song of innocence and freedom;
a mockingbird themed Beatnik vision.

You were set apart, set free and muted too soon.
Your trapeze pants, long hair and large-brimmed hats
a mirror of independence
 from the long night's reign of fear.

You were looking for Xanadu
and you found Xanax
like in-between angels at the end of days
becoming numb on the tepid waters
of relief from everlasting pain.

Geronimo

Her grey sweater
soaking wet on the white skin
glistening with drops of celestial water
singing in tune to the Geronimo song.

A night to remember on the frozen
by the derelict Hungarian palace.

They made rhymed puns
their thoughts hanging on a golden wreath.

Geronimo, she said,
and he whispered Mongols' rides,
from here to the incomparable,
the broken analogy,
the weaving closeness
of two parallel
          lines.

Immaculate Conception

If God were a seamstress,
she'd borrow her clothes
from the Salvation Armyof dreamers
who toil in those mists of metaphor,:
immaculate conception of the world.

Our parched hills
would be like gossamer robes
on the shoulders of children ... evanescent,
like the first idea that bred the first word.

Janice Jamboree

She sang her best blues song
hailing with the son of a preacher man
from afar never got close enough
for the sedate heart
for the monotonous life.

Jumbled words jamming the traffic
of close-knit souls
consuming like a blaze
of vaporous fumes
the weight of land,
the weightlessness of sound.

Until a blast emerged immaculate
and composed an unfazed blown-up voice
that they heard up in the heavens,
an Orpheus in trapeze jeans
and tie-dyed, hippie shirt:
a matchless soul that was sold
for priceless ransom of tears.

Janice jamboree:
the world turned inside out
like in a carnival of words
that flew beautiful
from her blessed mouth
and encircled the world
in a green wreath
of lost love and angel tears.

What David Said

He split himself
into three quiet magi
who sang the fourth and the fifth ...
a hallelujah for the sinners and the mad.

He was one, but divided,
like Osiris' limbs shattered over the plains
that an unwilling Isis gathered
in her city of music and words.

What David said when he saw her
was a droplet of blood falling
on the unwritten page
that undressed the moon
like a blank cocoon.

And he sang all his love
and sorrow and tribulations
and the three magi wept on the silver screen
beside themselves in a dustbin of amber
entranced and submissive like déjà vu.

What David , and she listened with care,
was a story that no man had dared tell before
about a time when love was pure and immense ...
bigger than butterflies' wings
and stronger than the soul's universe.

www.ingramcontent.com/pod-product-compliance
Lightning Source LLC
Chambersburg PA
CBHW071357200726
48294CB00004B/1203